HELLO, I'M THEA!

I'm *Geronimo Stilton*'s sister. As I'm sure you know from my brother's bestselling novels, I'm a special correspondent for *The Rodent's Gazette*, Mouse Island's most famous newspaper. Unlike my 'fraidy mouse brother, I absolutely adore traveling, having adventures, and meeting rodents from all around the world!

The adventure I want to tell you about begins at Mouseford Academy, the school I went to when I was a young mouseling. I had such a great experience there as a student that I came back to teach a journalism class.

When I returned as a grown mouse, I met five really special students: Colette, Nicky, Pamela, Paulina, and Violet. You could hardly imagine five more different mouselings, but they became great friends right away. And they liked me so much that they decided to name their group after me: the Thea Sisters! I was so touched by that, I decided to write about their adventures. So turn the page to read a fabumouse adventure about the

THEA SISTERS!

colette

She has a passion for clothing and style, especially anything pink. When she grows up, she wants to be a fashion editor.

Paulina

Cheerful and kind, she loves traveling and meeting rodents from all over the world. She has a magic touch when it comes to technology.

Violet

She's the bookworm of the group, and she loves learning. She enjoys classical music and dreams of becoming a famouse violinist.

THE THEA SISTERS

Nicky

She comes from Australia and is very enthusiastic about sports and nature. She loves being outside and is always ready to get up and go!

Pamela

She is a great mechanic: Give her a screwdriver and she'll fix anything! She loves pizza, which she eats every day, and she loves to cook.

Do you want to help the Thea Sisters in this new adventure? It's not hard — just follow the clues!

When you see this magnifying glass, pay attention: It means there's an important clue on the page. Each time one appears, we'll review the clues so we don't miss anything.

ARE YOU READY?
A NEW MYSTERY AWAITS!

Thea Stilton

AND THE
BLACK FOREST BURGLARY

Scholastic Inc.

Copyright © 2017 by Edizioni Piemme S.p.A., Palazzo Mondadori, Via Mondadori 1, 20090 Segrate, Italy. International Rights © Atlantyca S.p.A. English translation © 2019 by Atlantyca S.p.A.

The publisher does not have any control over and does not assume any responsibility for author or third-party websites or their content.

GERONIMO STILTON and THEA STILTON names, characters, and related indicia are copyright, trademark, and exclusive license of Atlantyca S.p.A. All rights reserved. The moral right of the author has been asserted. Based on an original idea by Elisabetta Dami. www.geronimostilton.com

Published by Scholastic Inc., *Publishers since 1920*, 557 Broadway, New York, NY 10012. SCHOLASTIC and associated logos are trademarks and/or registered trademarks of Scholastic Inc.

Stilton is the name of a famous English cheese. It is a registered trademark of the Stilton Cheese Makers' Association.

This book is a work of fiction. Names, characters, places, and incidents are either the product of the author's imagination or are used fictitiously, and any resemblance to actual persons, living or dead, business establishments, events, or locales is entirely coincidental.

ISBN 978-1-338-54698-9

Text by Thea Stilton
Original title *Il segreto della foresta nera*
Art director: Iacopo Bruno
Cover by Caterina Giorgetti, Flavio Ferron
Illustrations by Barbara Pellizzari and Flavio Ferron
Graphics by Alice Iuri / theWorldofDOT

Special thanks to Kathryn McKeon
Translated by Anna Pizzelli
Interior design by Kay Petronio

10 9 8 7 6 5 4 3 2 1   19 20 21 22 23

Printed in the U.S.A.   40
First printing 2019

OPERATION VACATION!

It was the end of the fall term at MOUSEFORD ACADEMY and the Thea Sisters were super excited. They had spent the last few weeks studying for exams, and it was time for a much-deserved vacation!

That morning, the sisters gathered in Colette and Pamela's room to discuss their trip. They still needed to buy **PLANE** tickets, make hotel reservations, and pack their suitcases.

But first, they needed to make the most important decision . . .

WHERE TO GO!

"Why don't we take a tour of the most popular winter FLEA MARKETS?" Colette suggested, looking up from Paulina's tablet. "This site says that there are tons of places to visit."

"FABUMOUSE idea!" Paulina replied enthusiastically.

"Or we could go skiing in the Swiss Alps. I could test out my skills on a black diamond," Nicky suggested.

"Or I could test out this new swimsuit at an ISLAND RESORT," Violet added, holding up her new purchase.

"What do you think, Pam?" Nicky asked her friend, who was busy fixing Violet's ALARM CLOCK.

"Hold on, I'm almost done . . ." Pam replied, tightening the last screw.

"Okay, your clock is ticking," she said,

passing the device to her friend.

"You're the best, Pam!" Violet squeaked, happily giving her a WARM hug. She was thrilled that her friend had been able to fix the old alarm clock. It had sentimental value. The clock had been a gift from her dear GRANNY when she went off to school and reminded her of home.

"Squeaking of ticking clocks, we better get moving on our vacation plans," Colette insisted. "Time is running out!"

"Coco's right, it might even be too late to make reservations," Paulina agreed.

Right then Pam's cell phone vibrated in her pocket. She pulled it out and checked her notifications.

"Holey cheese, talk about timing!" she squeaked, staring at an email.

Then she began reading the email aloud.

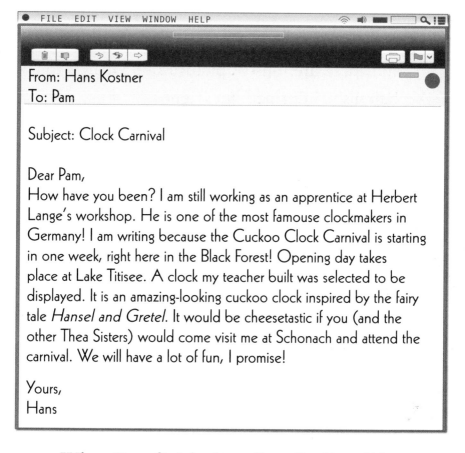

FILE   EDIT   VIEW   WINDOW   HELP

From: Hans Kostner
To: Pam

Subject: Clock Carnival

Dear Pam,
How have you been? I am still working as an apprentice at Herbert
Lange's workshop. He is one of the most famouse clockmakers in
Germany! I am writing because the Cuckoo Clock Carnival is starting
in one week, right here in the Black Forest! Opening day takes
place at Lake Titisee. A clock my teacher built was selected to be
displayed. It is an amazing-looking cuckoo clock inspired by the fairy
tale *Hansel and Gretel*. It would be cheesetastic if you (and the
other Thea Sisters) would come visit me at Schonach and attend the
carnival. We will have a lot of fun, I promise!

Yours,
Hans

When Pam finished reading, Paulina did a
quick search on her tablet.

"Oh my goodmouse! The **Black
Forest** sounds amazing according

to this travel site! The forest looks magical and there are tons of picturesque villages to visit," she informed her friends.

"Does it say anything about the carnival?" Nicky asked.

"Yes, apparently it's a big event, with clock exhibits, folk dancing, and food stands with local delicacies."

"I'd love that!" squeaked Violet and Nicky together.

"Me too!" added Colette, grinning excitedly.

"Black Forest . . . here we come!" Pam exclaimed.

She typed out a quick response to Hans as Paulina booked everyone tickets for a flight to Germany.

Meanwhile, the rest of the Thea Sisters **sprang** into action. Now that they knew where they were going, they could start packing their bags.

Excited squeaks filled the room. The Thea Sisters were off on another

MOUSERIFIC ADVENTURE!

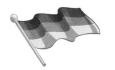

WELCOME, THEA SISTERS!

A few days later, the Thea Sisters boarded their flight bound for the B l a c k F o r e s t.

After takeoff, Paulina pulled out her tablet and started reading aloud about the airport and their first destination: **FREIBURG**.

"Do you mouselets want to hear something interesting? It says here that we are landing at the only tri-national airport in the whole world."

"What does that mean?" Pamela asked, confused.

"Well, it says the airport was built by Switzerland on French territory, but it also services the town of Freiburg, in Germany."

Listen to this . . .

"**COOL!** It's like going to three different countries at the same time," her friend noted.

"What's the plan after we land? How long will it take to get to **FREIBURG**?" Colette chimed in.

Paulina explained that they would board a bus when they arrived at the airport that would take them on an hour-long ride to the city of **FREIBURG**. The sisters were thrilled they would have time to check out the countryside as soon as they arrived.

Twenty minutes later, the mouselets stared out the bus windows, MESMERIZED by the dense woods and snow-covered peaks on the ride to Freiburg.

"It's like being in a *fairyland*!" Violet exclaimed.

"You said it, Vi!" Colette joined in. "**Cheesecake!** This is going to be one fabumouse vacation! Did you know this area is referred to as Baden-Württemberg?"

"Yes, this is a state of Germany!" Pamela said.

Transfixed by the incredible scenery, the time *FLEW* by and soon the bus was pulling into the station.

The Thea Sisters were welcomed by the sun shining warmly in a cloudless blue sky.

"I read that Freiburg is also called the **SUNNY** city. Now I know why!" Violet exclaimed, a smile on her snout.

"How funny, the **Gasthaus*** that Hans recommended has something to do with the sun, too," Pam explained. "It's called **SONNENSTRAHL**, which in German means 'ray of sun.'"

Paulina typed the address of the guesthouse into her cell phone, then led the way through the immaculate streets. The Thea Sisters love walking through the places they visit. Its the best way to really see the sights. The streets were lined with bright, **COLORFUL**, Bavarian-style buildings.

"Everything here is so neat and clean," Violet observed, admiring the houses and

*_Gasthaus_ means "guesthouse," or a small inn.

their windows, adorned with lovely curtains and **FLOWERPOTS**.

When they reached a sunny **YELLOW** house with **teal** shutters, Paulina said, "This is it! This is where we'll be staying!"

"Oh, how cute!" Colette gushed, clapping her paws.

FREiBURG, THE JEWEL OF THE BLACK FOREST

The sisters were delighted to discover the guesthouse was as inViting on the inside as it was on the outside. After depositing their bags, the mouselets relaxed in a charming, flowery sitting room with warm cups of herbal tea.

"Is everyone ready for some sightseeing?" Violet asked a while later after they finished their drinks.

"How about we check out the old town and the CATHeDRAL first?" Paulina suggested, reading from her guidebook.

"Good idea," Pam replied, unfolding the tourist map the owner of the guesthouse gave them. "I know we have our smartphones, but this map clearly indicates all the important sights, as well as the train and bus stations."

"LOOK, our guesthouse is marked, too!" Violet said, pointing to it on the map.

"Perfect!" Pam continued. "We'll have no problem finding our way back home. Let's go!"

Pulling on their coats, the Thea Sisters scurried outside into the bustling streets, ready to explore.

"Hmm . . . what smells so good?" Pam asked, sniffing the air. She headed toward a small food stand in the corner of a C O B B L E S T O N E square.

Paulina flipped through the pages of her guidebook. "Here it is! I knew I saw a picture of them. What you are SMELLING is the traditional German and Austrian **PRETZEL**," she said, reading aloud.

"Pretzels! I love pretzels! And these look whisker-licking delicious!" Pam declared, making a beeline for the stand. She returned a few minutes later holding a bag with two large, warm, FRAGRANT pretzels.

"Try it; it's still hot and delicious!" she squeaked.

The mouselets each tried a piece of the pretzel and agreed with their friend. It was YUMMY!

Munching on the pretzels, the sisters continued exploring the quaint little streets.

Suddenly, Nicky noticed something UNUSUAL.

"Is that running water?" she asked, pointing to a small canal in the middle of the street.

"What is it? It continues past the corner," Paulina noted. "Let's check it out."

"Wait a minute, I remember an **article** I read in the guidebook about these canals.

They look delicious!

They're called **BÄCHLE**, which I think means —" Colette began.

"'Narrow streams!'" Paulina interrupted her, reading from her tablet.

"And if I remember correctly, they were built in the Middle Ages to bring water to town," Colette continued.

Paulina nodded her head in agreement. "That's right, Coco!" she exclaimed. "They are now a **FAMOUSE** Freiburg landmark."

The Thea Sisters walked along the *Bächle* for a bit and noticed that other tourists were doing just the same. Some young mouselets were even having fun FLOATING toy boats in them!

Eventually, the mouselets reached a majestic cathedral positioned in the middle of the square.

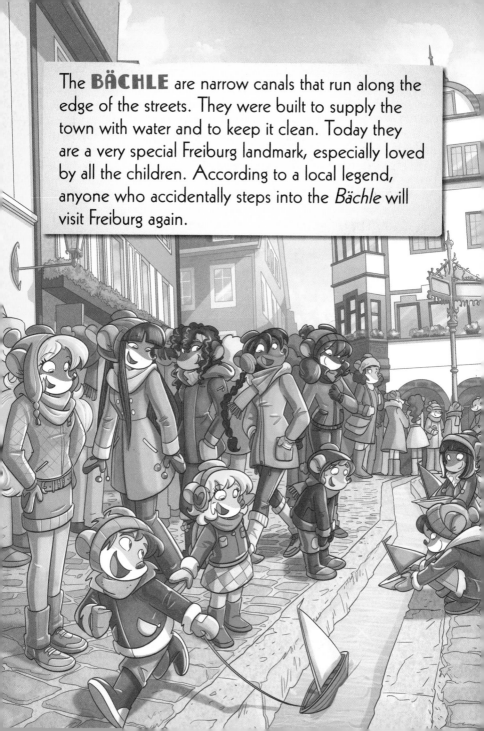

The **BÄCHLE** are narrow canals that run along the edge of the streets. They were built to supply the town with water and to keep it clean. Today they are a very special Freiburg landmark, especially loved by all the children. According to a local legend, anyone who accidentally steps into the *Bächle* will visit Freiburg again.

"Holey cheese! That is so impressive!" Pam exclaimed, her eyes SHINING as she stared up at the imposing building.

Paulina wasted no time and started SNaPPiNG pictures. The Thea Sisters would never forget this incredible day!

FREIBURG

The Cathedral

Freiburg's Cathedral is a clear example of a huge Gothic church. It is so big that it took 350 years to build it!

The Histonsches Kaufhaus

The Kaufhaus is a historic merchants' hall. Every day, a flea market takes place in the square opposite it.

Then . . .

. . . time for a rest and a delicious meal!

HERBERT LANGE, MASTER CLOCKMAKER

After a good night's sleep, the Thea Sisters woke up the next day full of energy. They couldn't wait to continue their exciting trip to the Black Forest.

"Hans just texted me. He says if we want, we can take the BUS to Schonach to meet him," Pam said.

"Perfect! I'll download the SCHEDULE on my tablet," Paulina replied.

Throwing on their warm coats, the mouselets chatted happily as they headed for the bus station.

As promised, as soon as the mouselets got off the bus, Hans was waiting for them.

"PAM! It's so great to see you again!"

Hans exclaimed with a **BIG** smile on his snout. "And these must be your friends, the THEA SISTERS!"

"I'm Colette, and this is Nicky, Violet, and Paulina," Colette squeaked, introducing herself and her friends.

We are the Thea sisters!

Hi, Hans!

Welcome!

Hans led Pam and her friends toward the workshop where he was working as an apprentice.

Schonach was a lovely little village surrounded by snow-covered mountains. Although the winter sun was shining brightly, a cold wind greeted the mouselets.

"BRRR!" Colette remarked, huddling in her jacket.

"It is colder here than in FREIBURG," Hans explained. "But don't worry. We are almost there!"

Herbert Lange's workshop was at the very end of a steep little street up a hill.

When the group finally reached the top, they couldn't help but notice the breathtaking view of the village and valleys below.

"Here we are!" Hans declared, ushering the Thea Sisters into the workshop.

"**WOW**, this place is busy!" Nicky observed as tourists spilled in and out of the shop.

"It's because of the carnival. Everyone in town knows that one of Master Lange's **CLOCKS** was picked to be displayed on inauguration day, and many fellow townsrodents are coming to congratulate him," Hans explained.

"**Holey cheese**, how many clocks are in here?" Pam asked, her eyes nearly **POPPING** out of her snout.

"About a hundred," Hans replied. "As soon as they are made, we hang them up to be sold."

"I **LOVE** this one with the dog!" Violet exclaimed, walking closer to get a better look.

Hans blushed. "Thanks! I actually made that one."

Right then a **gruff** voice called out, "Hans, there you are! I have been looking for you! I need you to pack this clock for the carnival. I have something **important** to take care of."

The friends turned to see the master clockmaker himself, Herbert Lange, staring at Hans and looking a bit **frazzled**.

"Of course, Herbert!" Hans answered before introducing the Thea Sisters.

"**Congratulations** on your clock!" Colette squeaked.

"Um, well, yes," Herbert muttered, barely acknowledging Hans's friends.

Instead, he directed his **gaze** at Hans.

"Hans, I'm trusting you with the clock," he warned before he abruptly *SCAMPERED* off.

How odd. The Thea Sisters weren't used to being snubbed. But before they could ask Hans about it, he said, "**FOLLOW ME!**"

Get the clock ready!

HANSEL AND GRETEL'S CLOCK

Hans led the mouselets to Lange's private **workshop** to see the famouse Hansel and Gretel clock.

"Your teacher isn't exactly the **chatty** type," Pam whispered to Hans, hoping the clockmaker was long out of earshot.

"Herbert doesn't have the best social skills," Hans consented. "But he is a skilled **builder** of cuckoo clocks."

Standing in front of the **magnificent** clock, the Thea Sisters had to agree.

"It must have been a really **LONG** and **COMPLEX** project," Nicky commented.

"When you have a PASSION, nothing is too complicated," Hans replied.

The Thea Sisters SILENTLY nodded.

Hans was right, because the same was true for all of them as well. They each had something they loved to do more than anything in the world.

Hans told the mouselets that Herbert had been inspired to make the Hansel and Gretel clock by the famouse *Grimms' fairy tale*.

What a project!

It's magnificent!

Amazing!

Apparently the fairy tale takes place in the Black Forest.

"But every cuckoo clock has its own story, with a miniature world made up of its own characters, objects, and special details," the ratlet concluded.

"Wow! Does that mean that there are no two cuckoo clocks that are the same?" Pam asked, amazed.

Hans nodded his head. "That's right. Each and every piece attached to the clock is carved by paw with UNIQUE features that match perfectly with that particular cuckoo clock," he replied.

For a moment, Hans seemed lost in thought, staring at the MAGNIFICENT cuckoo clock with admiration in his eyes. Then the young clockmaker asked another apprentice to help him pack up the clock.

The Thea Sisters **WATCHED** in silence while the ratlets wrapped it up.

First, they wrapped the clock in a large white fleece blanket. Then they wrapped it in bubble wrap and carefully taped it. Then they carefully placed it in a box.

Careful . . .

Finally, the two apprentices DELICATELY laid the clock inside a wooden box.

"All done!" Hans declared, pleased with his work. "Franz, can you tell Herbert that the **HANSEL AND GRETEL** clock is safely packed and that I will be meeting him here tomorrow morning to seal the box?"

After Franz left the room, Hans turned to Pam and her friends. "Tomorrow morning, we can leave all together for Lake Titisee. As for tonight, I booked a room for you at a really nice Gasthaus nearby," he said.

The Thea sisters were thrilled they would get to spend more time with their new friend Hans. And they couldn't wait for the carnival!

"And I have an even bigger surprise," Hans continued. "How would you like to see an

ENORMOUSE cuckoo clock? It's right here in Schonach. We can actually walk around **INSIDE** the clock!"

"We'd love to!" the Thea Sisters squeaked.

It's a huge clock!

Wow!

INSIDE A CUCKOO CLOCK!

The group walked around and took in some of the sights. Hans led the Thea Sisters through downtown *Schonach* until they reached what appeared to be a cottage with a **GIANT** clock face in the center.

"Is this really a clock? From here, it just looks like a house . . ." Nicky noted.

"Wait until you see the inside. I am so excited to show you! It looks like you are standing inside a real working clock!" Hans explained. "Come on, I'll show you!"

Pam was the first to step inside the clock house. *Holy cheese!* The sight left her SQueaKLeSS!

All the gears of a regular clock were there, but they were much **BIGGER**!

"Wow! This is amazing!" Paulina squeaked, looking around.

"I have always thought so," Hans said. "It's one of my favorite places. The clockmaker and owner of this house took three years to make it."

"**Unbelievable!**" Nicky chimed in.

"Let's go outside to look at the cuckoo!" Violet suggested.

Everyone went outside except for Pam, who was getting very close and inspecting the gears trying to figure out how they worked. She was fascinated!

At seven sharp, the cuckoo POPPED out of the window. The Thea Sisters jumped back a bit, startled by the size of it.

"That's one big bird!" Colette observed.

"That's amazing," Violet squeaked. "I read in one of the guidebooks that this is not the only cuckoo that is so large."

"You are absolutely right. There is one other cuckoo clock that also has a huge bird. That clock is in the village of Triberg, and it's also impressive. The paw-carved cuckoo bird is more than fourteen feet long and weighs more than three hundred and thirty pounds!" Hans explained. "If you have some extra time, you might want to take a trip there to take a look. It really is a sight to see."

Right then a cold wind ruffled everyone's fur.

"Brr," Colette said, shivering. "It's getting pretty chilly." Hans could see that the mouselets were starting to shiver a bit, so the group headed back to the *Gasthaus*. As they walked they were treated to the **magical** sight of fresh

snowflakes drifting down from the sky.

WE'RE READY FOR THE CARNIVAL

The following day, the village of Schonach woke up to a soft blanket of snow.

The Thea Sisters had a healthy breakfast, then waited outside the *Gasthaus* for Hans to pick them up.

Nicky stared at the snow with a twinkle in her eye. She quickly made a **snowball** and took aim at Pam, who was checking her phone.

"Who did that?!" Pam squeaked, whirling around with a laugh and spotting Nicky. "You're in for it now, sister!"

Pam threw a snowball at her, which **barely** missed her. Nicky made another one and aimed for Paulina, who was all set up for battle.

"I'm not **PLAYING**! I don't want to get my fur wet . . ." Colette began to say, when a snowball hit her.

She stood silently in shock for a moment. The other mouselets tried to muffle their

Hey!

My fur!

squeaks of laughter. Eventually, she gave in and joined the fight.

Soon the mouselets were engaged in an all-out, honest-to-goodmouse **snowball fight**. When Hans arrived at the *Gasthaus,*

Gotcha!

he saw the mouselets covered in snow, with snouts red from the cold, happily hugging and laughing.

Herbert, who was driving, stared at them in silence. How awkward.

The Thea Sisters quickly shook the snow off their coats and climbed into the van. Hans greeted his friends warmly, but Herbert didn't squeak a word. Could it be that he disapproved of snowball fights? Or maybe he just didn't like the mouselets?

Luckily, Hans chatted away excitedly to his friends, distracting the mouselets from Herbert Lange's strange behavior.

After about an hour, the Thea Sisters saw a sign for the town of Titisee. Suddenly, the most amazing view spread out before them. It was a picturesque town on a half-frozen

lake, surrounded by snow-covered **PINE FORESTS**. The mouselets couldn't take their eyes off the magnificent sight.

The **Black Forest** was full of surprises, one after another!

"It's beautiful here, isn't it?" Hans asked them. "We are so used to this view, but it leaves an impression on anymouse who sees the **frozen** lake for the first time."

Paulina nodded while snapping pictures.

"Can you ice-skate on it?" Nicky inquired

"In some parts, yes, you can," the ratlet replied.

"I would like to try!" Nicky exclaimed.

"Me too, even though I'm no **expert**," Pam squeaked.

Then Herbert spoke for the first time, instructing Hans to finish unloading the **CLOCK** before he went skating.

"Of course, I definitely will, Herbert." Hans nodded.

The van drove **FARTHER** into downtown Titisee, which was decorated with snowy trees, and a thousand glittering lights hanging on the streetlamps.

Finally, Herbert pulled over outside a big building, with a RED-and-GOLD banner that read, Cuckoo Clock Carnival.

"This is the carnival headquarters," Hans declared. "The Hansel and Gretel clock will be displayed here."

Right then two strangers came out of the building and greeted Herbert and Hans.

Herbert introduced them as Gustav and Bert, members of the Cuckoo Clock Carnival planning committee.

They both helped unload the *delicate* clock from the van.

"Let's put it over here," Herbert said, POINTING to a spot next to the largest pedestal in the hall. Then he took some tools from a toolbox to remove the clock from the box.

The whole room grew silent in anticipation.

THE GUEST OF HONOR WAS ABOUT TO BE REVEALED!

A TERRIBLE
SURPRISE

Even though the Thea Sisters had already seen the **HANSEL AND GRETEL CLOCK**, they were still excited and couldn't take their eyes off the wooden box. The clock was one of a kind, and they couldn't wait to see it on display.

With **CAREFUL** paws, Herbert eased open the box and with his helpers laid it on the pedestal. Then they unwrapped the protective layers around the clock.

"What a **MOUSTERPIECE**!" Gustav exclaimed, eyes shining.

Herbert beamed, filled with pride over his creation. But as quickly as his smile appeared, a second later it **disappeared**. A look of **HORROR** replaced it.

"B-b-but this can't be!" he squeaked, turning completely red in the snout.

"What is it, Master?" Hans asked, worried.

"THE WITCH! SHE DISAPPEARED!"

Herbert replied.

Hans immediately checked the base of the clock. He rubbed his eyes twice before admitting the awful truth: The witch figurine was gone.

"I don't know what happened . . ." Hans mumbled, shaking his snout in shock.

"I trusted you!" Herbert exploded, GLARING at Hans.

"I don't understand. When I packed the clock, everything was in order," Hans said in DISBELIEF.

"Maybe the figurine fell off when you were packing it?" Pam said, trying to help.

"Good idea, Pam. We could check the fleece blanket that was used to WRAP the clock," Nicky added.

"If we can't find it, maybe we can substitute it with another one," Paulina offered.

By now, Herbert's fur was *standing* on end. "That witch was stuck on! It did not just fall off!" he squeaked furiously. "And no, we can't replace it with another one.

"The witch is an essential part of the clock, and it must be the original one. If not, the clock cannot qualify for the opening ceremony."

In fact, without Herbert's magnificent **HANSEL AND GRETEL** cuckoo clock, the whole Cuckoo Clock Carnival event would need to be reorganized.

"Herbert, is there anything I can do?" Hans asked sadly.

"You did plenty already. I trusted you with the clock, Hans. I am very disappointed in you," the master coldly replied.

Hans hung his head as Herbert STORMED out of the room.

"Oh, Hans, we all saw how carefully you packed the clock," Paulina said, trying to make him feel better.

Pamela began RUMMAGING through the box that had held the clock. Suddenly, she let out a squeak. "Hey, there's something here!"

"Is it the witch?" Hans asked hopefully.

"No, it's a **SILVER BUTTON**," Pam replied.

"Maybe it belongs to whoever stole the witch figurine!" Paulina speculated.

MOLDY MOZZARELLA! The missing witch figurine was turning into a real mystery!

Just then Hans, who had

A button?

been closely inspecting the wooden base of the clock, shook his head. "This is strange," he muttered, a puzzled expression crossing his snout.

"**WHAT?**" Pam inquired.

"Look at this. This is where the witch was glued," he explained, pointing to a spot.

"You can barely see it," Colette observed.

"Exactly, which makes me think that the figurine was taken out by someone who knew exactly what they were doing, like a craftsmouse clockmaker," he replied.

The Thea Sisters nodded in agreement. Only a rodent who knew the fine art of clock making would have been able to REMOVE the witch figurine without a scratch to the delicate cuckoo clock.

"And even more than damaging the clock, the thief wouldn't want to damage the figurine. After all, **stealing** the witch was the original plan!" Colette concluded.

CLUES!

ONLY AN EXPERT CRAFTSMOUSE COULD HAVE TAKEN THE WITCH CAUSING NO DAMAGE.

SOMEONE'S SILVER BUTTON WAS IN THE BOX THE CLOCK WAS PACKED IN... COULD IT BELONG TO THE THIEF?

A FRIEND IN NEED

Unfortunately, knowing the witch had most likely been stolen by a seasoned clockmaker didn't make Hans feel any better. Herbert had put him in charge of protecting the clock and he had **BLOWN** it. He felt like the security mouse at a bank who falls asleep in the middle of a **cat burglary**.

"The witch disappeared under my watch. Herbert is right to be upset with me," Hans groaned, **PACING** back and forth.

"Don't beat yourself up, Hans," Pam advised. "This is not your fault."

A minute later, Herbert stamped back into the room. "I am going back to *Schonach* to search the workshop. Maybe I can find some clues that will help me figure out who stole my precious figurine right out from under someone's snout!" he announced, shooting Hans an ANGRY look.

Hans stared at the floor, mortified.

"I am SORRY, Master Lange. You have every reason to be UPSET; however, what happened is not Hans's fault," Paulina exclaimed, jumping to the ratlet's defense.

It's not Hans's fault!

"You don't understand. No one here understands," Herbert sniffed.

"What do you mean?" Pam asked.

"That witch was a one-of-a-kind figurine, ONE OF A KIND," he repeated to stress the importance of that statement.

The Thea Sisters and Hans looked at one another. What could they say? Hans had already explained that each cuckoo clock was unique, but Herbert was acting like they were CLUELESS.

Still FUMING, he went outside and boarded the van headed back to Schonach.

No one squeaked.

Finally, Pam spoke up. "Well, what do we do now?"

"How about we go sit somewhere WARM so we can think this through?" Violet suggested.

Everyone agreed getting Hans away for a

little bit seemed like a ratastic idea, so they pulled on their warm coats and headed into town. It didn't take long for the mouselets to settle into a booth at a cozy tearoom nearby.

"These hot cheddar scones are whisker-licking delicious!" Pamela squeaked, biting into her third cheesy treat. "Take them away, before I eat them all!"

Hans and the rest of the Thea Sisters broke into laughter, and soon they were all happily squeaking away about everything and anything . . . except cuckoo clocks! The sisters were relieved to see their new friend's mood improved. Unfortunately, it didn't last long.

Right then the cuckoo clock in the tearoom struck the hour, abruptly bringing everyone back to reality.

"I have to find that witch figurine or the whole Cuckoo Clock Carnival will be ruined . . . all because of me!" Hans lamented, tugging nervously at his whiskers.

"Why does Herbert keep saying that we don't understand the significance of the missing figurine?" Colette wondered aloud.

Here it is!

Oooh...

Hans explained that when Herbert first came up with the idea to build the Hansel and Gretel clock, he said he was inspired by a precious witch figurine.

"Let me guess, it was the same witch statue that DISAPPEARED," Pam suggested.

Hans nodded. "Exactly. He told me that the figurine was one of a kind. Unique, old, and precious."

"Therefore, if I understand you correctly, the witch figurine was not **specifically** made for this clock," Violet reasoned.

"No, it's much **older**. And Herbert did not make it."

"So who made it?" Paulina asked.

"I don't know; Herbert never told me," Hans replied.

"Hmmm . . . this is getting more and more complicated . . ." Nicky mumbled.

"But it seems that the key to solving this mystery all revolves around this mysterimouse FIGURINE."

Hans closed his eyes as if trying to make the missing figurine magically appear. Suddenly, he sat up straight and blinked. "I just thought of something!" he squeaked. "It might not mean anything, but I remember there was a stamp at the base of the witch statue!"

He took a pen from his pocket and began drawing on a paper NAPKIN.

Villingen

"**Villingen?**" Colette read when he showed them the drawing.

"It's another town in the Black Forest . . ."

"And it's a great clue we can use to start our **investigation**!" Pam declared.

CLUES!

THE FIGURINE WAS NOT CARVED BY MASTER LANGE AND IS QUITE OLD. WHO COULD HAVE CARVED IT?

THE BASE OF THE FIGURINE HAS A VERY PARTICULAR STAMP, WITH THE WORD "VILLINGEN."

TRACKING DOWN THE WITCH

The Thea Sisters agreed the best place to get more information on Villingen was, of course, in the town itself!

"Road trip!" the mouselets squeaked in unison.

"How will we get there?" Paulina asked, ready to search on her TABLET.

"I'll borrow Bert's car," Hans replied. "In fact, my cousin Greta lives in the town of Villingen. She moved there to open a bakery. She can help us investigate!"

"Perfect!" Colette replied.

"Perfect that she owns a bakery, too . . ." Pam squeaked, already **dreaming** of the delicious desserts they might discover.

Hans chuckled as he assured the mouselets

that his cousin was a truly fabumouse baker. "Wait till you try her Black Forest Cake!" he squeaked.

"Black Forest Cake?" Pam inquired. "I never heard of it."

"Something tells me that's about to change!" Colette giggled, eyes twinkling.

It's a very yummy cake!

Yippee!

Before long, Hans and the Thea Sisters found themselves back on the road on another mouserific adventure! **Destination: Villingen!**

With their snouts pressed closely to the windows, the mouselets were blown away by the unbelievable view. Wide-open valleys and *jagged* mountains covered in snow were in stark contrast to the dense **MYSTERIMOUSE**-looking woods.

"Wow! This place is *spectacular!*" squeaked Nicky in appreciation.

"I am happy you like it!" Hans replied. "I purposefully picked this route so that you could *ENJOY* the unique scenery of this area."

"It is all worth it!" Paulina confirmed.

A little while later, the group arrived in the town of Villingen.

Hans parked the car and the group began

walking toward the downtown area. As they walked, Hans explained that Villingen was the site of the first **watch factory** in 1858 and an extraordinary *clock mouseum*.

"I'd **LOVE** to visit!" Pam squeaked.

Everyone agreed that the **mouseum** was a must-see, but first they needed to get cracking on the case.

Here is the bakery!

Just then the group arrived in front of a beautifully **decorated** store window. "This is my cousin's bakery," Hans announced.

When they got closer, however, the mouselets saw a note on the door. It read:

"Rats!" Violet squeaked. "What are we going to do now?"

"Let's wait for a little bit . . ." Colette suggested.

After a few minutes, though, the group grew tired of waiting. The **cold** air **ruffled** their fur, and still there wasn't a rodent in sight.

To pass the time, Paulina began looking up information on the **WITCH STAMP** on her tablet.

"I'm not finding anything," she sighed.

"Hey, I've got an idea!" Colette suddenly squeaked up. "How about we go check out the *Clock Mouseum*? Maybe we can find some useful **information** there!"

"Good idea," Hans replied. "If the stamp is **famouse**, they will know all about it."

DiFFiCULT RESEARCH

The Clock Mouseum was located in an old building right in the center of Villingen. When the group arrived at the entrance, the door was open, so Hans and the mouselets stuck their snouts inside and squeaked loudly, "Hello! Anybody here?"

An older rodent with gray fur appeared behind one of the display cases. He was holding a brush in his right paw and a can of wax in this left paw.

"Good afternoon, mouselets. I am sorry, but the mouseum is closed today," he said.

The KIND caretaker explained that the group would need to return the next day if they were interested in a tour.

"Thank you very much," Hans replied. "But

we are not here to visit the **mouseum**."

"We are looking for information on a **STAMP**," Colette added.

"What kind of stamp?" the caretaker asked, **CURIOUS**.

We are looking for information . . .

"This one," Hans said, showing him his napkin drawing. "It was carved on the bottom of a FIGURINE that was made for a cuckoo clock."

The caretaker put his tools down and peered at the napkin. "Well, would you look at that!" he exclaimed.

Strange . . .

"Do you recognize it?" Paulina asked, hopeful.

"But of course! It is a very famouse old stamp. In fact, some of our OLDEST clocks on exhibit have that very same stamp."

"REALLY? Can you show us one?" Nicky asked excitedly.

The caretaker led the mouselets into the next room. He opened a display case and took out a small cuckoo clock with SHEPHERD and sheep figurines.

"These figurines are CARVED so perfectly!" Hans commented. "Look at the intricate details of this little lamb."

"You certainly know what you are squeaking about, young rat," the caretaker said, smiling.

He wasn't surprised when Pam pointed out that Hans was studying to be a clockmaker.

"Then you must know ANTON KELLER," he remarked.

Hans scratched his snout. "The name sounds familiar . . ."

"KELLER made the most amazing clocks," the caretaker explained. Turning the clock around, he added, "Here is his stamp."

"Oh my goodmouse! That's it!" Paulina exclaimed.

Hans and the Thea Sisters could hardly contain their excitement. Now all they had to do was find Anton Keller!

Unfortunately, the caretaker explained that Keller had retired many years ago.

"But perhaps you can go speak with George Ziegler. He's another craftsmouse clockmaker who now works in Keller's old workshop. Maybe he can help you," the caretaker suggested.

"Is his workshop in Villingen?" Colette asked.

Nodding, the older rodent scampered over to a small desk and began rummaging through the drawer. "Ah, here it is!" he squeaked, holding up a business card and handing one to Colette. The card read: George

Ziegler, master clockmaker, Villingen.

"Thank you, you have been most helpful!" Hans exclaimed, waving good-bye.

GEORGE ZIEGLER

Master Clockmaker

Villingen

The group returned to the street in great spirits. The investigation was on!

THE COLLECTOR

George Ziegler's workshop was right around the corner, not far from Hans's cousin's bakery. The bell above the door JANGLED as the friends scurried inside. Holy cheese sticks, the place was TICKING! Cuckoo clocks of every size and shape covered the walls, each with their own musical ticktock.

Just then a craftsmouse wearing a blue WORK APRON appeared. "Hello, how can I help you?" he squeaked politely.

"Hello, we are looking for George Ziegler," Hans told the mouse.

"That would be me!" the rodent replied.

The group quickly explained the purpose of their visit. While the mouselets were SQUEAKING, George listened attentively. It seemed George had, in fact, purchased

the workshop from Anton Keller not that long ago. But when he heard that the mouselets were **SEEKING** information on a figurine carved by Keller, his eyes OPENED wide.

"Well, isn't that a strange coincidence," he said, stroking his fur. "I haven't heard Keller's name since I bought this place and now I've been asked **twice** about his figurines in the same week!"

"Really?" Paulina asked, curious.

"Yes, a stranger came in and asked about his old cuckoo clock and carved WOODEN figurines," he replied.

What were the chances that another rodent would be searching for Keller's figurines? The Thea Sisters agreed; the cuckoo clock mystery was getting more interesting with every ticktock of the clock!

After the stranger's inquiry, Ziegler said he unearthed a couple of Keller's figurines. "He

offered me a **large** sum of money, so I sold them," the rodent continued. "I figured he was probably a **collector.**"

"What kind of figurines were they?" Hans asked, a serious look on his snout.

"A female mouse wearing a traditional dress and a **LUMBERJACK** with a bundle of wood on his shoulders," Ziegler replied.

"I wish we could have seen them," Nicky lamented.

"Oh, but you can!" the craftsman assured them.

Apparently, Anton Keller had meticulously cataloged his work by taking **pictures** of each and every piece. Ziegler left the room and returned a few minutes later carrying a stack of **dusty** record books.

He set them on the counter and started going through them. "Here they are," he said, showing them two pages from one of the books.

"Keller's work is **extraordinary**," Hans commented, looking closely. "But it is really weird that a stranger would buy these FIGURINES right now."

"If you think about it, the whole story is strange. First Lange's witch disappears, then a mysterimouse collector goes looking for Keller's old figurines . . ." Nicky recapped.

"Could you describe what the collector looked like?" Colette asked.

"Um, he was **TALL** . . . I can't remember his snout well . . . he might have had a beard, or no, maybe a **mustache** . . . I'm sorry, I see so many rodents each day," Ziegler confessed.

Without a better description, the chance of finding the stranger seemed hopeless. Then Ziegler remembered one important detail. The stranger had been dressed in an *expensive*-looking jacket that was **MISSING** a button.

Hans and the Thea Sisters exchanged *excited* glances. Ziegler had no idea but he had just given them hope in

SOLVING THE MYSTERY!

CLUES!

THE COLLECTOR WHO BOUGHT THE TWO WOODEN FIGURINES CARVED BY ANTON KELLER WAS WEARING A JACKET THAT WAS MISSING A BUTTON! COULD IT BE THE SAME SILVER BUTTON THAT WAS FOUND IN LANGE'S CLOCK BOX?

NOW YOU'RE
SQUEAKING!

When Ziegler stopped squeaking, Colette told him about the button they had found in Herbert Lange's box after UNPACKING the Hansel and Gretel cuckoo clock. Hans pulled the button out of his pocket and showed it to the clockmaker.

The craftsmouse looked at it closely as the mouselets held their breath. Finally, he announced, "Yes, I believe this is the same button. It is quite unique."

"Maybe the collector went to *Schonach* to look for other Anton Keller figurines," Colette guessed.

"And maybe it was him who stole the witch," Paulina whispered.

The mouselets had a lot to think about now

that they had possibly discovered where the missing button had originated. Hans suggested they discuss the case further over a delicious slice of Black Forest Cake at his cousin's bakery.

"Now you're squeaking!" Pam agreed, picturing herself nibbling on the sweet treat in the cozy bakery.

Thanking Ziegler for his help, Hans passed the record book back to the craftsman. It was then that he noticed a second name on the cover of the book. It read: Herbert Lange!

To the mouselets' amazement, Ziegler explained that Herbert Lange was one of two apprentices at Anton Keller's shop. He showed them a picture of Herbert in the book.

"**IT'S HIM!**" Paulina cried.

"Do you know him?" Ziegler asked.

"I am the apprentice in his workshop, in Schonach," Hans replied.

Suddenly, it was crystal clear as to why Herbert was so fond of the witch figurine . . . it was carved by the man who trained him!

"Why not ask Lange about Keller's work?" Ziegler suggested.

Hans shook his snout. If only it were that simple. Unfortunately, he told the mouse, Herbert was an intensely *private* rodent.

The more Hans thought about his master's silence, the worse he felt. Why hadn't Herbert told Hans he had worked for the famouse Anton Keller? After all, an apprentice's job was to learn everything about his craft. Ziegler had also told the mice that the other apprentice in Anton's workshop was named Josef Schutzen. But Herbert had never mentioned him. **WHY?**

The mouselets thanked Ziegler for his help and left the shop feeling even more confused. To 𝓵𝓲𝓰𝓱𝓽𝓮𝓷 the mood, Pam linked paws with

He never talked about it . . .

Hans and declared, "Come on, everyone! It's time for cake!"

Following their friend's lead, the Thea Sisters resolved to put the mystery on hold as

It's time for cake!

they headed past quaint shops and stores on their way to the bakery. And sorting out the clues to the mystery would surely be much easier after a slice of Black Forest cake!

CLUES!

HERBERT LANGE WAS ONE OF ANTON KELLER'S APPRENTICES BEFORE THE MASTER RETIRED.

THERE WAS ANOTHER APPRENTICE, JOSEF SCHUTZEN, BUT LANGE NEVER TALKED ABOUT HIM . . . WHY?

CAKE, CAKE, AND MORE CAKE!

When they arrived at Hans's cousin's bakery, Pam stopped. Cakes, chocolate pastries, and fruit tarts were delicately displayed on shelves and cake stands in the bakery window.

"Holey cheese! What a view!" Pam exclaimed. "Everything looks so YUMMY! I might never leave!"

The Thea Sisters and Hans erupted in laughter.

Still cracking up, the group entered the bakery and was immediately enveloped in

Yummy desserts!

the sweet, comforting aroma of homemade pastries.

A young mouselet with a long blond *braid* appeared from behind a flower-printed curtain.

What a nice surprise!

"Greta!" Hans shouted.

"Hans! What a nice surprise!" she replied, a wide grin spreading across her snout.

"I'm sorry I didn't have a chance to let you know we were coming. These are my friends Pam, Colette, Nicky, Paulina, and Violet."

Greta welcomed the Thea Sisters to her bakery with open paws.

"Congratulations, Greta. This place is

MOUSERIFIC!" Pam squeaked, admiring the tastefully decorated shop with its CHEERY paint, sleek counters, and cozy tables.

Greta smiled. "How about a SWEET TREAT while you tell me the reason for your visit?"

"Definitely!" they replied, eagerly climbing onto stools at the counter.

Disappearing behind the curtain, Greta returned shortly with a large chocolate cake topped with cherries.

"This is the typical dessert from this area in Germany. It's called Black Forest Cake, just like the forest," she explained.

"It looks DELICIOUS!" Colette exclaimed.

"Believe me, it is," Greta confirmed, cutting slices and serving them to her guests.

"This is the BEST cake I ever had!" Paulina squeaked.

Black Forest Cake

It was created in the Black Forest, and it first appeared around 1930. It was inspired by the traditional black costume the local ladies wear: black with white blouse and headdress with red pom-poms, just like red cherries.

"Can I have another piece, please?" Pam asked. "I want to remember the flavor. Maybe we can make it when we get back to **MOUSEFORD ACADEMY**."

Colette WINKED at Pam. The mouselets glanced at each other and giggled.

"Okay, okay, I'm really having another

slice because it's so **fabumouse**!" Pam confessed, chuckling.

In the meantime, Hans filled Greta in on the details of their trip including the missing WITCH FIGURINE, the SILVER BUTTON, the Clock Mouseum, and George Ziegler's shop.

"I know Ziegler well—he is very **KIND**," the cousin nodded.

"He was very helpful," Paulina agreed. "He told us about a mysterimouse collector who has been looking for old figurines **CARVED** by Keller."

"And we found out that Keller was Lange's master, but he never told me about it," Hans went on, a worried look on his snout.

"There had to be some connection between the carved FIGURINES, the mysterimouse collector, Keller, and his old apprentices . . .

Herbert Lange and Josef Schutzen," Paulina mused out loud.

"You mean, in addition to the STAMP?" Hans asked, pulling the paper napkin with his drawing from his pocket and setting it down on the counter.

Greta LOOKED at the napkin carefully. "Oh my goodmouse!" she squeaked, jumping up. "I can't believe it! I have definitely seen this before. It's identical to the stamp of an old cuckoo clock I saw not too long ago at the Baden-Baden baths. I remember my friend who works there pointed it out to me!"

"It must be another ANTON KELLER clock!" Violet squeaked.

Apparently, the clock in Baden-Baden wasn't WORKING well, Greta explained, and the shop was looking for an expert to FIX it.

"Looks like we just figured out our next stop," Pam announced, swallowing her last piece of cake.

"Baden-Baden!" the Thea Sisters agreed, inviting Greta to join the search.

OFF TO BADEN-BADEN!

Early the next day, the Thea Sisters and Greta scampered to the train station and waited for the train departing for BADEN-BADEN. Hans accompanied the mouselets to the station, but he had decided not to join them on the excursion.

"Are you sure you don't want to come?" Greta asked Hans as the train rolled up to the gate.

"Yes, I have a lot to do here. Plus, I have to think things through and I want to call Herbert. Maybe he will tell me more about his former colleague Josef Schutzen," he said.

The mouselets boarded the train, which left a little while later. Pamela and Greta stood by the window to wave good-bye to Hans.

"Well, even if we don't find any clues, we can still check out the Baden-Baden **thermal baths** I read about," Colette suggested.

"Oh yes, the baths are mouserific!" Greta confirmed.

After a pleasant trip through the **beautiful** snow-covered German

See you soon!

Good luck!

countryside, the train arrived at the Baden-Baden station. Stepping off the train, Greta and the Thea Sisters were greeted by icy snowflakes and a **cold**, *biting* wind.

"Brrr, it's **freezing**!" Paulina exclaimed.

"One more reason to visit the warm **baths**!" Greta squeaked as she led her new friends through the streets of **BADEN-BADEN**.

"It's so pretty!" Violet exclaimed, looking around. Sturdy, **bright** lanterns hung from **festive** garlands between the many shops and buildings. And there were lots of restaurants, cafes, and bakeries crowded with tourists squeaking happily.

"How magical!" Nicky exclaimed.

"It is magical! Especially because of the thermal **baths**!" Greta replied, stopping in front of an impressive building with **TALL** windows.

"Here we are! These are the famouse Friedrichsbad Roman-Irish **baths**, built in 1877!"

"**Fabumouse!**" Violet said.

"Wait until you go inside!" Greta exclaimed, ushering the mouselets into the building.

"I think we are in for the perfect stress-busting afternoon!" Colette squeaked excitedly.

Here are the baths!

Fabumouse!

WHAT A DELIGHTFUL SCENT!

As soon as the mouselets stepped into the entrance to the baths, they were enveloped by the sweet scent of flowers and warm vanilla.

"It smells like heaven in here!" Violet squeaked, lifting her snout and SNIFFING the air.

Greta nodded, explaining that the thermal baths used only natural oils and salts.

Then she scampered to the reception desk, where she asked if she could squeak with her friend.

"Of course, let me get her for you right away," the receptionist squeaked pleasantly.

The receptionist returned with another mouselet by her side. "Hi, Greta, what a nice surprise!" the mouselet squeaked, hugging her friend. The pin on the mouselet's uniform read Anita.

"I'm so sorry I didn't call first," Greta apologized, returning the hug.

"No worries. You know you can come anytime!" Anita replied warmly.

Greta introduced the Thea Sisters one by one. Then she explained how the mouselets were there to attend the Cuckoo Clock Carnival that was starting in two days.

Greta, what a surprise!

"The problem is we have to solve a mystery before then, and we need your help," Greta went on, a serious look on her snout. Anita's eyes grew **larger** as Greta filled her in on the missing witch figurine and the strange Anton Keller stamp.

"Wow, this is a real **mystery**!" Anita exclaimed.

"Yes, it is. And if we don't solve it soon, the carnival will be ruined." Greta sighed, chewing her whiskers.

Anita wasn't sure how she could help the mouselets with their **investigation**, but she quickly assured them she was on board.

"Fabumouse!" Colette squeaked. "We would like to take a look at your **cuckoo clock**. Greta told us she saw one here."

"Hmmm . . . the only cuckoo clock we have is in the back office," Anita remarked.

"I remember you showed it to me a couple of months ago," Greta squeaked.

"That's right! Follow me!" Anita led her

friends through the hallways.

They finally arrived in a small room with a cuckoo clock hanging on one wall.

"It's completely white!" Pam exclaimed, surprised.

Completely white . . .

Strange . . .

"And completely DiFFeReNT than what we have seen so far," Colette added.

"As far as I know it's supposed to be quite old. That's the reason why it sometimes doesn't work," Anita explained.

In fact, the Thea Sisters learned that just the previous week the cuckoo clock had been packed up and sent out for repairs. Gathering around the precious antique, the mouselets carefully compared the stamp on the back of the clock with the ANton KeLLeR drawing.

"Yep! It's a real Keller all right!" Colette confirmed, pointing. "The stamp is identical!"

"Anita, you just said the clock was recently fixed," Paulina remarked. "Do you know who repaired it?"

Anita shook her snout but offered to check the payment records for the name of the repairmouse.

The Thea Sisters watched as Anita went to a file cabinet in the corner of the room and PULLED out the drawer. She took out a folder filled with what appeared to be bills and payments. Then she began sorting through them one by one. "Here it is!" she squeaked at last, holding up a piece of paper. "Let's see . . . the clockmaker who repaired this was a mouse named JOSEF SCHUTZEN."

His name is Schutzen . . .

"Oh my goodmouse! The same apprentice who WORKED for Anton Keller!" Paulina told Anita.

The sisters quickly filled Anita in on their suspicions. Josef Schutzen just might be the mysterimouse collector!

"We need to squeak to Schutzen as soon as possible!" Pam cried.

Luckily, the clockmaker's address was listed on the invoice Anita had pulled from her files. He lived in the town of Triberg, a picturesque village known for its world famouse waterfalls.

"Wow! Can't wait to see them!" Nicky exclaimed, RUBBING her paws together in anticipation. It was no secret: Nicky loved the OUTDOORS almost as much as freshly baked CHEESECAKE!

The sisters agreed they would continue their **investigation** in Triberg, but first they would return to Villingen to pick up Hans and fill him in on their findings.

"Before you leave, how about a dip in one of our THERMAL POOLS?" Anita suggested.

"Count me in!" Colette replied.

The rest of the Thea Sisters readily agreed, and soon they found themselves relaxing like pampered mice in a LUXURIOUS outdoor thermal pool. Ah!

Nothing like a warm bath surrounded by cold snow!

INFORMATION EXCHANGE

After the relaxing baths, the Thea Sisters boarded the train back to Villingen with renewed energy.

"I'm glad we followed Anita's suggestion," Paulina exclaimed.

"You said it!" Violet squeaked. "A WARM pool in the middle of snow-covered country was really magical!"

For a while, the sisters mused about their day at the baths and the other beauty treatments offered at Baden-Baden.

"Maybe someday we can return to try them out again," Colette sighed.

As the train carrying the Thea Sisters CHUGGED farther and farther away from the station, the mouselets' thoughts returned to the **mystery** of the missing figurine. It didn't seem likely that Hans's master, Herbert Lange, would suddenly start SQUEAKING about his past. Herbert was a mouse of few words. Still, there must be a secret to uncover . . .

Before long, the train arrived at its destination and the mouselets scampered out into the cold night air, heading straight for Greta's cozy apartment. The hot steamy baths of Baden-Baden seemed a distant memory as they CRUNCHED through the icy snow.

"Welcome back!" Hans exclaimed when at last the mouselets burst through Greta's front door. "I was just putting the kettle on to make some hot tea. Would you like me to make you some?"

"Oh, yes, please!" the mouselets replied at the same time, shrugging off their heavy winter jackets.

They couldn't wait to tell Hans what they had found out.

"So Josef Schutzen is still working in the **B l a c k   F o r e s t**!" Hans squeaked after the mouselets had updated him.

"That's right, and he repairs Anton Keller's clocks," Colette replied.

There was a long **MOMENT OF SILENCE**, after which Greta asked her cousin, "Did you call Herbert Lange?"

"Yes, I did." Hans nodded, scratching his head. "He was still very **UPSET** about the **MISSING** witch. I asked him about Josef Schutzen, and he acknowledged that they once worked together in Anton Keller's worshop."

Still, Hans reported, Herbert Lange clammed up completely when the ratlet attempted to ask him any more questions. He would only say that he had not heard from Schutzen in a long, long time. The whole thing was rather odd.

"Perhaps, though, if we find Schutzen, we might be able to find out more," Hans suggested.

"One step ahead of you, Cousin!" Greta giggled. "Anita helped us get Schutzen's address. He lives in **Triberg**!"

Hans grinned. Now they were getting somewhere! Triberg was only a couple of hours away! With renewed excitement, the mouselets made a plan to leave for Triberg early the next morning.

As snow drifted down from the starry skies, the friends spent the evening squeaking around a COZY fire. The mouselets and the mystery were finally heating up!

A JEWEL OF A TOWN

The following morning, the Thea Sisters, Greta, and Hans left for Triberg. As soon as they arrived, the mouselets agreed it was a **breathtaking** town. Triberg was located in a valley lined by green hills. The *lush* forest surrounded the houses like a thick, protective blanket.

Like all the other towns on the clock route, the whole town was festively decorated with lights and garlands strung everywhere.

"These towns are so beautiful!" Colette observed.

"Uh-oh. Look at the sky," Paulina noted, staring at the **thick** clouds. "I think it's about to snow."

Not wanting to get stuck in a snowstorm, the mouselets got down to business.

"Let's try that store," Pam suggested, pointing to a clock shop across the **square**. "Maybe they know Josef Schutzen."

"Good idea. I am sure Schutzen is well known in town since he repairs clocks," Nicky said, hopeful.

Inside the store, the mouselets were greeted by the **SWEET** smell

of wood and varnish and soft, CHEERFUL music. A shopkeeper wearing a traditional Black Forest costume welcomed them and asked if she could help.

"Good morning, madame. We are looking for some information about a clockmaker," Hans began.

"Well, you are in the right place," the shopkeeper replied, smiling.

"His name is JOSEF SCHUTZEN," Pam clarified, stepping forward.

Upon hearing that name, the shopkeeper's eyes opened wide. "Oh my goodmouse! I haven't heard that name in a long, long time!" she squeaked.

She explained that many clockmakers lived in Triberg, but Josef Schutzen was not one of them. "He lives a very QUIET, secluded life and rarely comes into town," she told the mouselets.

How strange. If Schutzen was such a recluse, it was hard to believe he had traveled all the way to Baden-Baden to fix the cuckoo clock at the thermal baths. Perhaps the broken clock was mailed to his address? The more the Thea sisters discovered, the more QUESTIONS they seemed to have!

"I think we will just have to visit Josef Schutzen at his home," Pam declared.

"Good idea," Nicky agreed, turning to the shopkeeper. "Do you know know how to get to his house?"

The good news was the shopkeeper gave them directions to Josef Schutzen's home. The bad news was he lived in a small wooden cottage in the middle of nowhere!

"Take the Path at the end of this street. It leads straight to the waterfall. Cross the bridge and continue on until you see a small clearing in the WOOdS," advised the shopkeeper.

The mouselets said good-bye and scurried out into the square. Following the directions, they soon found themselves on the path that LED through the woods.

PROGRESS REPORT!

THE MYSTERIMOUSE COLLECTOR IS VERY INTERESTED IN MASTER ANTON KELLER'S FIGURINES.

ANTON KELLER HAD TWO APPRENTICES, HERBERT LANGE AND JOSEF SCHUTZEN, WHO ARE NO LONGER IN TOUCH.

JOSEF SCHUTZEN LIVES IN A HOUSE IN THE WOODS AND HAS RECENTLY FIXED A KELLER CLOCK DISPLAYED IN THE BADEN-BADEN BATHS.

THE HEART OF THE BLACK FOREST

The group of friends trudged through the dense woods in a single line. The cold air smelled of pines and bark as light snowflakes **DRIFTED** down from the sky. They were cold and out of breath, but they didn't care one bit!

"What a **MOUSERIFIC** place!" Nicky exclaimed. "It's like a **fairyland**!"

Eventually, the steep path changed into a gentler uphill, lined by rocks and lumpy tree trunks.

It's so beautiful!

"Sometimes, when you see a place often, you forget how magical it really is. The Black Forest has been the inspiration for some of the most world-famous FAIRY TALES.

And many **movies** are filmed here,"
Hans squeaked as they walked.

"This place is so QUIET . . ."
Violet noted, staring at the trees
looming around them. The forest
felt so mysterimouse. It was almost
as if the trees were **guarding** old

It is almost
scary . . .

secrets. ". . . and a little bit SPOOKY, to be honest!" she finished, whiskers beginning to tremble.

"Oh come on, Vi, don't be so silly. WHAT COULD HAPPEN? We are all together!" Pam soothed, trying to calm her friend.

These are very old trees . . .

"I'm only saying I would hate to get lost out here on my own," Violet responded.

Right then a heavy clump of snow fell from the branches of a tree. The mouselets jumped with fright.

"It's just a tree saying hello," Hans joked.

Everyone burst out **laughing**.

A few minutes later Colette heard another sound. "Do you hear that?" she asked.

"It sounds like water," Nicky guessed, while Hans and Greta exchanged a knowing look.

The amazing Triberg waterfalls were just a few pawsteps away.

Hans and the mouselets stopped right by the wooden bridge that looked out over the falls.

Together the group stood admiring the soft WHITE FOAM that erupted from the flowing water.

"Wow. This is amazing!" Violet said.

"You can certainly say that Josef Schutzen did not pick an **ordinary place** to live," Nicky noted.

"It's a bit isolated for me," Colette replied.

"He must be a **SPECIAL** rat," Greta went on.

"Well, you could say Herbert is, too," Hans supposed. "I wonder if their particular ways kept them from being good **FRIENDS**. I am very curious to know more about their past as Keller's apprentices."

On that note, the friends agreed it was time to pick up the pace. If the snow continued **FALLING** at this rate, they might have trouble on the return trip.

The mouselets crossed the bridge and continued following the path, sticking close together. Before long, they reached a small

clearing with a LITTLE WOODEN cottage at its center. White smoke BILLOWED from the chimney.

"Here we are," Hans said. "This must be Josef Schutzen's house."

THE WINTER FOREST CLOCK

Once they reached Schutzen's house, the Thea Sisters and their friends stood still for a moment, holding their breath, full of EXCITEMENT. They were about to meet a very talented mouse who might be able to help them solve their big mystery! The snow falling from the sky was the only thing moving.

"What do we do? Should we knock?" Colette suggested.

Hans and the mouselets took a few PAWSTEPS to the door. They knocked a few times, but nobody answered. Colette, Hans, and Greta peeked through a window.

The others did the same, looking through a side WINDOW.

"There's no one home," Hans said.

Suddenly, a voice from behind them said, "Who are you? What are you doing here?"

Hans, Greta, and the Thea Sisters whirled

Who are you?!

around to discover a stranger wearing a heavy winter jacket and wide-brimmed hat. He had a beard and in one paw he clutched a bundle of sticks.

"Oh, we are terribly sorry . . . we do not mean to disturb you . . ." Hans started saying.

"Well, you did," the stranger muttered. "Please leave."

"Sorry, it's just really important that we find Josef Schutzen," Violet explained. "We have some questions we would like to ask him."

Just then, a GUARDED look came over the stranger's snout.

"We just need to have a quick chat with him," Greta squeaked. "About some figurines carved by Anton Keller. We're sure he would want to help us."

Finally, Pam *blurted* out, "Are you Josef Schutzen?"

The master clockmaker stood SILENTLY for a few moments, then at last nodded. "It's me," he said, walking to the door. "You might as well come in. Please wipe your wet shoes on the porch."

Hans and the mouselets looked at one another, stomped the snow off their paws, and followed Josef Schutzen inside.

The house was very simple, but clean and well kept. A wood stove was on, GENTLY WARMING the air. There were beautiful clocks hanging on many of the walls.

"Please, sit down," Josef said, taking off his jacket and hat. He offered his guests some tea.

After the **LONG** trek through the snowy forest, the Thea Sisters were **happy** to sip the delicious hot tea.

In the meantime, Hans was looking around for clues that might connect Schutzen to Herbert Lange or Anton Keller.

"Are you working on a new clock?" Hans asked, noticing a workbench at the back of the room **covered** with a cloth.

"Can you show us?" Pamela asked, curious.

"Sorry, I couldn't. It isn't ready yet." Schutzen responded.

"That's okay, we aren't experts," Coco said, smiling. "But while we have been here we have seen some pretty amazing clocks. I bet yours is just as good!"

"Just as good?" Schutzen looked a bit uncertain but eventually he walked to the workbench and revealed an enormouse, stunningly beautiful cuckoo clock.

"I bet this is better. What do you think?" He asked **PROUDLY**.

The mouselets were squeakless as they studied the clock. It was incredible! It was set in a snowy landscape full of figurines, decorations, and details **carved** with the utmost care. There were two *beautiful* fairies holding up the face. And there was even a figurine that looked a lot like Josef himself.

Suddenly, Pam jumped up. "Holey cheese, those are the two figurines we saw in Ziegler's book! And that one . . . is Herbert's WITCH!"

At the same time, Colette looked at Josef's jacket, hanging by the door. It was missing a silver button!

Holey cheese! They had stumbled across the answer. Josef Schutzen was the thief of the witch figurine! But the **MYSTERY** wasn't completely solved yet. The friends needed to find out . . .

WHY?!

I Am the Thief!

The Thea Sisters and their friends couldn't take their eyes off Josef. They could hardly believe that the witch thief, the mysterimouse collector, and Anton Keller's apprentice were all the same rodent!

"How do you know about the witch?" Schutzen asked before anyone else could squeak a word.

"I apprentice for Herbert Lange," Hans firmly replied. "That FIGURINE belongs to the Hansel and Gretel cuckoo clock . . . and it was STOLEN!"

The master clockmaker turned PALE. With a bowed snout, he admitted he had taken the figurine.

"But why?" Colette asked.

"We already know you and Herbert were

apprentices at the same time. Weren't you friends?" Paulina continued.

A **nostalgic** look passed over Schutzen's snout. "Yes, we worked together in Villingen."

Opening a drawer, he pulled out an **OLD** photograph and showed it to Hans and the mouselets.

The two ratlets were watching Anton Keller work with **smiles** on their snouts. What made them stop squeaking to each other?

"We had different opinions about a certain issue . . . mostly about that clock," Schutzen admitted sadly, pointing to the piece.

The Winter Forest cuckoo clock was Anton Keller's most ambitious work. He had spent most of his life working on it.

When Anton retired, he left his clocks to Herbert and Josef. Schutzen wanted to finish

But the clock . . .

I am not interested . . .

the Winter Forest clock, but Herbert did not. The two argued, and things were never the same after that. The workshop closed and the mice went their separate ways.

"But you still wanted to finish it . . ." Pamela suggested.

"Yes, I kept all of the original plans for the clock," the older rodent admitted. "I created most of the decorations, but I wanted to get some of the original pieces."

"Like the WITCH," Nicky guessed.

The mystery was slowly coming together. But still something didn't make sense.

"Why didn't you just ask Herbert for the FIGURINE?" Hans asked.

The clockmaker admitted that had been his original plan. In fact, he had traveled to Schonach in order to talk to Herbert. But when he saw all of the excitement for the **HANſEL AND GRETEL** cuckoo clock, Schutzen quickly realized Herbert would think he was just jealous of the attention. He would never give up the witch.

"So you stole it," Paulina declared.

"And now, with no witch, the Hansel and Gretel clock cannot be displayed at the Cuckoo Clock Carnival," Colette pointed out.

Josef shook his head. "I know I've made a mess of things. But I don't know what to do. I can't remove the witch now that the Winter Forest clock is finished!"

Right then Hans had an idea. What if Josef took the clock to Titisee? Then everyone could see the amazing Winter Forest clock along with the **HANſEL AND GRETEL** clock!

As Schutzen considered the suggestion, the mouselets held their breath. If Josef agreed, then not only would the missing witch figurine make it to the carnival, but once there, the two mice could finally talk and maybe even reignite their friendship.

Josef agreed.

"**Hooray!**" the mouselets cheered.

HELLO, HERBERT . . .

When the group arrived at the Titisee Clock Great Exhibition Hall, it was clear that something was wrong. Worried, official-looking rodents SCAMPERED about squeaking into phones. Only then did Josef realize the problems he had caused by stealing the WITCH FIGURINE.

"Oh, dear, I am so embarrassed," he squeaked in despair. "I had no idea how important the carnival is for everyone."

"The important thing is that you are here," Hans replied. "We will find a SOLUTION!"

Right then Herbert walked in and SUDDENLY stopped right in his paw tracks in front of Josef. They stared at each other, squeakless, for a long, long, long moment as the Thea

Sisters watched in **nervous** anticipation.

Finally, Josef broke the silence. "Hello, Herbert, I owe you my **apologies** and some explanations, too," he confessed.

"Hello, Josef, I am very **surprised** to see you here," Herbert replied, *SHOOTING* a look at Hans.

"There is something I think you should see," Hans said softly.

Then, without another word, Hans and Josef began to carefully unpack the box containing the exquisite Winter Forest clock. Herbert watched the rodents' every movement with a **PUZZLED** expression. But his expression turned to complete shock when the contents of the box were finally revelead.

"I cannot believe it . . . the Winter Forest cuckoo clock!" Herbert exclaimed. "You actually made it—you finished our master's project!"

"You know how *important* it was to me," Josef replied.

"So much so that you STOLE that!" Herbert exclaimed, pointing to the witch figurine standing at the base of the masterpiece.

Josef knew the only way he could make things right was to return the figurine. So he carefully **unglued** the delicate wooden DECORATION and handed it to Herbert.

"I really am sorry, Herbert," he squeaked as the mouselets looked on, smiling.

The Winter Forest cuckoo clock!

As much as he wanted the witch figurine, Herbert realized the **PRECIOUS** piece truly belonged to the Winter Forest clock. After all, it was an Anton Keller original and taking it wasn't the right answer. After insisting Josef return the witch to its rightful place, Herbert grinned at his old friend.

"But what is going to happen to the **HANSEL AND GRETEL** clock?" Pam asked, worried.

"I will try to explain to the carnival organizers," Herbert replied. Then he turned to Josef. "You did a fabumouse job with our master's project. I'm sorry for not believing in you all those years ago."

The two friends shook paws, tears in their eyes.

"Hurray!!!" Greta, Hans, and the Thea Sisters rejoiced, cheering for the two old friends.

It seemed everything was working out. Well, almost . . . if only there were some way to display the **HANSEL AND GRETEL** clock. But without the **missing** piece, it seemed hopeless.

"Isn't there something that can be done?" Violet asked, disappointed.

"Yes, it's such an amazing clock. It deserves

You made this??

to be shown!" Colette chimed in.

Ever since the witch figurine went **missing**, Hans had been thinking about how he could help. There was only one solution. He would try to make a **REPLACEMENT**. Now he pulled the piece out of his pocket and presented it to Herbert.

"I know this is not nearly as **GOOD** as the Anton Keller piece, but maybe we could use this," he suggested nervously.

Herbert stared at the figurine. It was identical to the one that was **stolen**!

"You carved this?!" Herbert asked,

incredulous, turning the witch over in his paws.

"Yes, while I was in Villingen," Hans admitted. "I know it's not as SPECIAL but I was hoping . . ."

"Not as SPECIAL?" Herbert squeaked. "It's AMAZING, my dear ratlet!"

"I agree with my colleague and friend," Josef agreed, happily inspecting the figurine.

"FaNtaStiC!" Pam exclaimed as Greta proudly hugged her cousin.

WONDERFUL NEWS

When Bert and Gustav walked into the cuckoo clock Great Exhibition Hall later that day, they were surprised by the FESTIVE atmosphere. They were expecting to see a lot of disappointed snouts following the news of the **missing** figurine. Herbert quickly filled them in on what had happened and introduced them to Josef.

Then he showed them the Winter Forest clock. In the end, it was agreed that both clocks should be in the exhibit.

"The new FIGURINE is mouserific, and we want to display your fabumouse clock, dear Herbert!" Gustav concluded.

Upon hearing those words, everyone breathed a sigh of RELIEF.

Hans was so EXCITED that his work had

received such praise. In fact, he could barely believe his own ears. And then an even more amazing thing happened. Herbert turned to Hans and announced that the ratlet was ready to be promoted from *apprentice* to **full-fledged assistant**!

"Thank you, Herbert. I will not let you down!" Hans squeaked happily.

Let the celebration begin!

After that, Herbert insisted the mouselets take the rest of the day off.

"I heard you say you might want to go **ice-skating**?" Herbert exclaimed, winking.

"Come on, Hans, let's go!" Nicky said excitedly. She could not wait to put on her **ice skates**!

I will help!

"Okay, but if you need me, Herbert . . ." Hans protested.

"I can help him with anything he needs." Josef said.

"Go, you deserve it!" Herbert ordered, smiling.

While the mouselets headed to the **LAKE**, Hans thought about his master's change of heart. It was the first time he had seen Herbert **genuinely** happy.

"It's all because of you, Hans," Greta said.

"I couldn't have done it without your help," Hans replied.

"That's what 𝔣𝔯𝔦𝔢𝔫𝔡𝔰 are for!" Pam said, beaming.

Soon all seven mouselets were skating around the FROZEN lake, breathing in the clean pine-scented air.

"This is amazing!" Pam shouted right before losing her balance as she tried to skate backward. Hans, who was skating right beside her, was able to catch her.

"Are you hurt?"

You were amazing, Hans!

Cheers for friendship!

he asked her while holding her in his paws.

"No, I am okay! Th-thank you for CATCHING me," Pam thanked him shyly.

"You are welcome!" he replied, BLUSHING. Their friends couldn't stop smiling.

THE CUCKOO CLOCK CARNIVAL

The following day, the entire town was ready for the **Cuckoo Clock Carnival**, due to start in the afternoon.

Look over there!

As the Thea Sisters waited with the crowd, Colette could not take her **EYES** off two mouselets distributing event brochures who were wearing the traditional Black Forest costumes.

Come to the carnival!

"Wouldn't it be great to wear a traditional costume?" the mouselet squeaked.

"Hey, why don't we all wear the costumes? It will be fun!" Paulina suggested as her friends nodded in agreement.

"I am in, too, mouselets!" Greta said. "Follow me! I will take you to a very special store where you can find all the traditional costumes you want!"

The store was a small BOUTIQUE full of pawmade costumes, created by the local seamstresses. The Thea Sisters had a blast trying them all on. Then they each chose one, complete with the traditional headgear with red pom-poms.

When they were ready, they scampered to the square just in time for the carnival.

The carnival organizers and the town officials were standing on the stage and

behind them . . . two **MONUMENTAL**
cuckoo clocks were displayed!

"Wow! Is that the Winter Forest clock?"
Colette asked, surprised to see it displayed.

"The jury thought it was so **beautiful**
they decided to **display** it next to Herbert's,"
Hans replied, joining his friends.

The Thea Sisters smiled at one another. At

last the two clocks and the two ***friends*** were back together.

"Real friendship lasts furever!" Pam squeaked happily, **WINKING** at all her friends as the band announced the start of the Cuckoo Clock Carnival.

WHAT A PERFECT ENDING TO A PERFECT STORY!